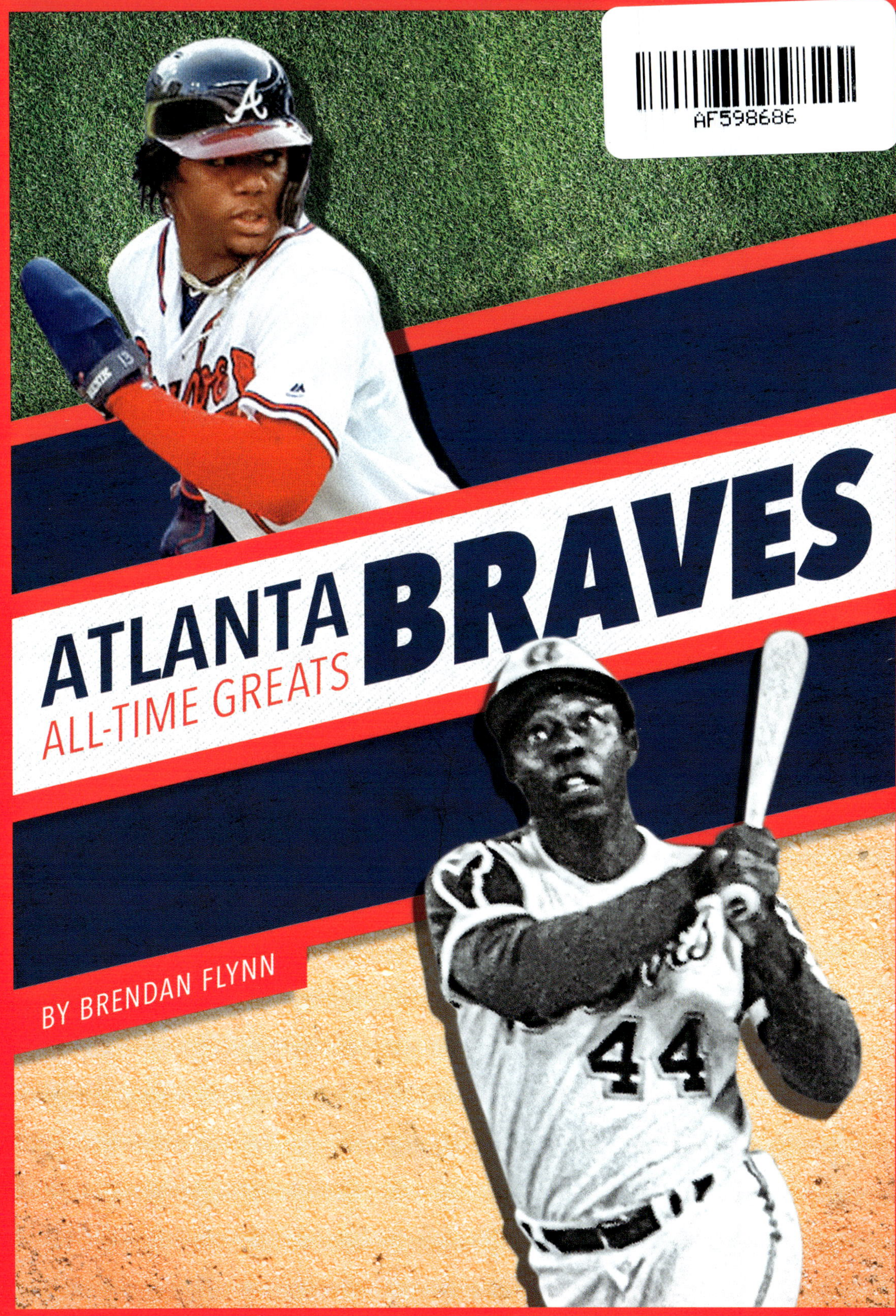

ATLANTA BRAVES

ALL-TIME GREATS

BY BRENDAN FLYNN

Book design by Jake Slavik
Cover design by Jake Slavik

Photographs © John Bazemore/AP Images, cover (top), 1 (top), 10; Harry Harris/AP Images, cover (bottom), 1 (bottom); AP Images, 4, 6; JMH/AP Images, 7; Bill Hudson/AP Images, 8; David Durochik/AP Images, 9; Eric Draper/AP Images, 13; Tom DiPace/AP Images, 14; Nick Wass/AP Images, 17; Charlie Riedel/AP Images, 18; John Minchillo/AP Images, 20; David Tulis/AP Images, 21; Red Line Editorial, 22

Press Box Books, an imprint of Press Room Editions.

ISBN
978-1-63494-289-8 (library bound)
978-1-63494-307-9 (paperback)
978-1-63494-343-7 (epub)
978-1-63494-325-3 (hosted ebook)

Library of Congress Control Number: 2020913878

Distributed by North Star Editions, Inc.
2297 Waters Drive
Mendota Heights, MN 55120
www.northstareditions.com

Printed in the United States of America
042023

ABOUT THE AUTHOR

Brendan Flynn is a San Francisco resident and an author of numerous children's books. In addition to writing about sports, Flynn also enjoys competing in triathlons, Scrabble tournaments, and chili cook-offs.

TABLE OF CONTENTS

AARON
44

CHAPTER 1

PIONEERS

The Braves are one of the oldest teams in the National League (NL). They began playing in Boston in 1876. They also played in Milwaukee, Wisconsin. They moved there in 1953. The next year, one of the greatest players in history made his debut with the Braves.

Hank Aaron was a skinny 20-year-old when he joined the Braves. He went on to break Babe Ruth's all-time home run record. Aaron set a record with 25 All-Star appearances. He hit at least 30 home runs in 15 seasons. And he was the NL Most Valuable Player (MVP) in 1957.

That year, Aaron and the Braves won the World Series. Two other Hall of Famers played on that team. Ace pitcher **Warren Spahn** won 363 games in his career. That's more than any other left-hander in history. He also won the Cy Young Award in 1957.

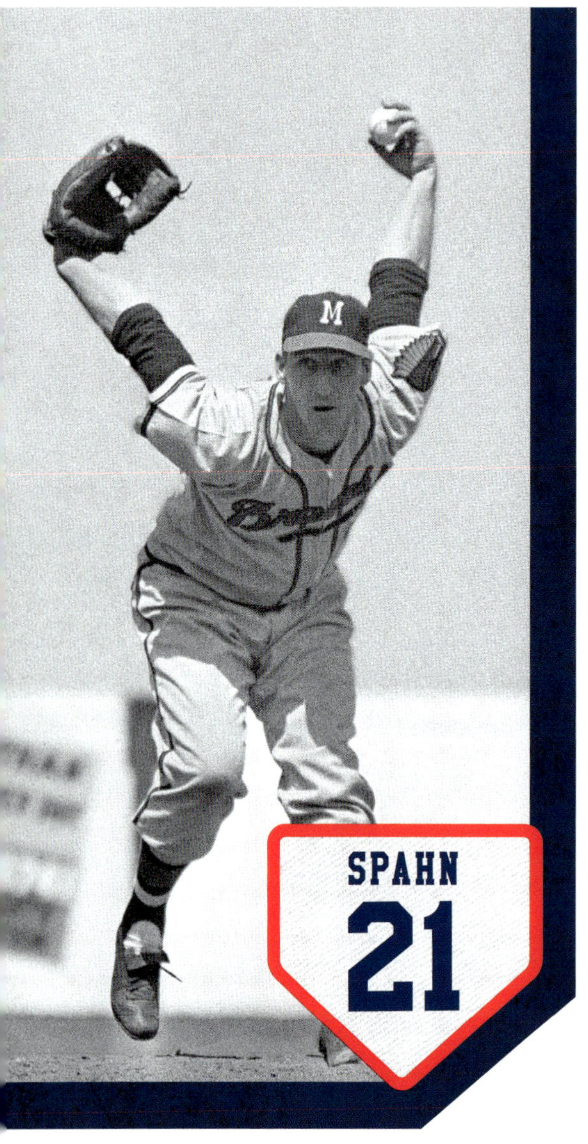

Third baseman **Eddie Mathews** was one of the most feared power hitters in the game. He and Aaron were a dangerous duo.

GREAT TIMING

Lew Burdette picked a good time to have the best week of his life. The right-hander won all three of his starts in the 1957 World Series. He threw a complete-game shutout in Game 7 at Yankee Stadium to clinch the title for the Braves.

Mathews was just the seventh major leaguer to hit 500 career home runs. He was a great fielder, too.

The team moved to Atlanta in 1966. They didn't have much success in those early years. But they did have some excellent players. Right-hander **Phil Niekro** baffled hitters with his knuckleball for 21 years with the Braves.

Only three pitchers in MLB history have thrown more than his 5,404 career innings.

Dale Murphy was one of the game's biggest stars in the 1980s. The slugging center fielder was named the NL MVP in 1982 and 1983. In each of those seasons, he hit 36 home runs

and led the NL in runs batted in (RBI). And he helped the Braves win the NL West in 1982. It was their only division title in a 21-year span.

STAT SPOTLIGHT

MOST CAREER PITCHING APPEARANCES

BRAVES TEAM RECORD

Phil Niekro: 740

SMOLTZ
29

CHAPTER 2
CLASSICS

Beginning in 1991, the Braves went on a remarkable streak. They won the division title 14 times in 15 years. The only year they missed was 1994, when the season ended early due to a labor dispute. Those teams won five NL pennants and the 1995 World Series.

Atlanta relied on some amazing pitchers during much of that streak. Braves starters won the NL Cy Young Award seven times in eight seasons. One of their best was right-hander **John Smoltz**. He came up big in pressure situations. Smoltz went 15–4 with a 2.67 earned run average (ERA) in the postseason.

Smoltz won the NL Cy Young Award when he led the majors with 24 wins in 1996. Six years later, as the Braves' closer, he led the majors with 55 saves.

Lefty **Tom Glavine** was one of the most reliable pitchers in Braves history. He averaged more than 16 wins per season from 1989 to 2002. And he led the NL in victories five times. Glavine almost never missed a start. He didn't throw hard. But he had pinpoint control. And he kept hitters guessing with a mix of pitches. Glavine won the NL Cy Young Award in 1991 and again in 1998.

STAT SPOTLIGHT

MOST CAREER STRIKEOUTS

BRAVES TEAM RECORD

John Smoltz: 3,011

GLAVINE
47

MADDUX
31

RULE CHANGES

The Braves' manager throughout their great run was **Bobby Cox**. The fiery Cox was a fan favorite. He managed the Braves for 25 seasons, interrupted by a four-year stint in Toronto and five years in the Braves' front office. Cox returned to the dugout in 1990, and Atlanta won five pennants over the next decade. His 2,504 career wins are fourth-most in MLB history.

Many people viewed **Greg Maddux** as a right-handed version of Glavine. He didn't overpower hitters with his fastball. He just outsmarted them. Maddux worked the corners of the plate as well as anyone in history. He also mixed speeds well. And he fielded his position, winning a record 18 Gold Glove awards. Maddux was named the NL Cy Young winner in four straight seasons from 1992 to 1995. The last three were his first three seasons with the Braves.

Of course, those great Braves teams had some great hitters, too. Third baseman **Chipper Jones** hit for both average and power. He spent 19 seasons in the big leagues, all with Atlanta. He retired in 2012 with a career .303 batting average. A switch-hitter, Jones was amazingly consistent. He hit .303 with a .405 on-base percentage (OBP) left-handed. As a right-handed hitter, he hit .304 with a .391 OBP. The 1999 NL MVP also blasted 468 career homers. He played with fire and determination that Braves fans loved.

Andruw Jones was a 19-year-old rookie starting outfielder in the 1996 World Series. He was known for making eye-popping catches and hitting long home runs. He led the majors with a team-record 51 homers in 2005.

C. JONES
10

A. JONES
25

ACUÑA JR.
13

CHAPTER 3

NEXT WAVE

The Braves won back-to-back division titles in 2018 and 2019. It was the first time they'd done that since their long streak ended in 2005. Like past championship teams, these Braves are led by a group of exciting players.

Ronald Acuña Jr. is one of the most dynamic talents in the game. His speed and power are a rare combination. He won the NL Rookie of the Year Award in 2018. The next year, he made his first All-Star team and finished fifth in MVP voting. Acuña led the NL with 37 stolen bases in 2019. He also slammed a team-leading 41 home runs.

Acuña teamed with second baseman **Ozzie Albies** to form one of the top young duos in the majors. Albies makes dazzling plays in the field. He also hits for power and average.

He hit 40 doubles and 24 home runs in each of his first two full seasons in the big leagues.

Veteran first baseman **Freddie Freeman** anchored the Atlanta lineup. The five-time All-Star was a consistent .300 hitter. He also provided leadership for his young teammates. And in 2021, Freeman helped the Braves win another World Series.

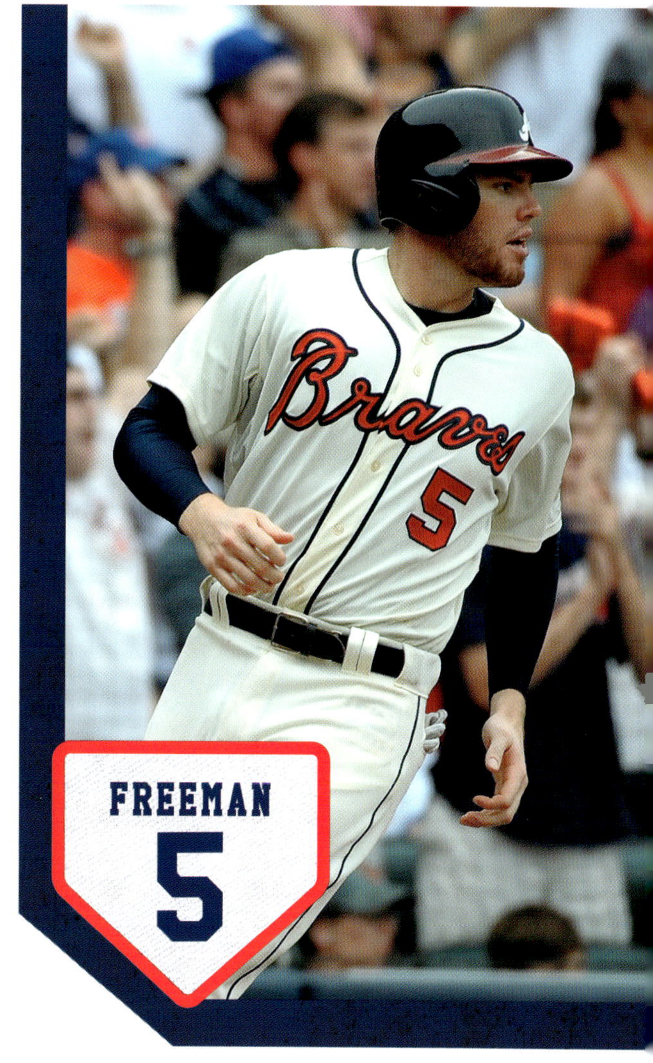

TIMELINE

1942
WARREN SPAHN
(1942, 1946–64)
1950
HANK AARON
(1954–74)
EDDIE MATHEWS
(1952–66)
1960
1970
PHIL NIEKRO
(1964–83, 1987)
1980
DALE MURPHY
(1976–90)
1990
TOM GLAVINE
(1987–2002, 2008)
JOHN SMOLTZ
(1988–99, 2001–08)
GREG MADDUX
(1993–2003)
2000
CHIPPER JONES
(1993, 1995–2012)
ANDRUW JONES
(1996–2007)
2010
FREDDIE FREEMAN
(2010–21)
RONALD ACUÑA JR.
(2018–PRESENT)
OZZIE ALBIES
(2017–PRESENT)
2020
2022

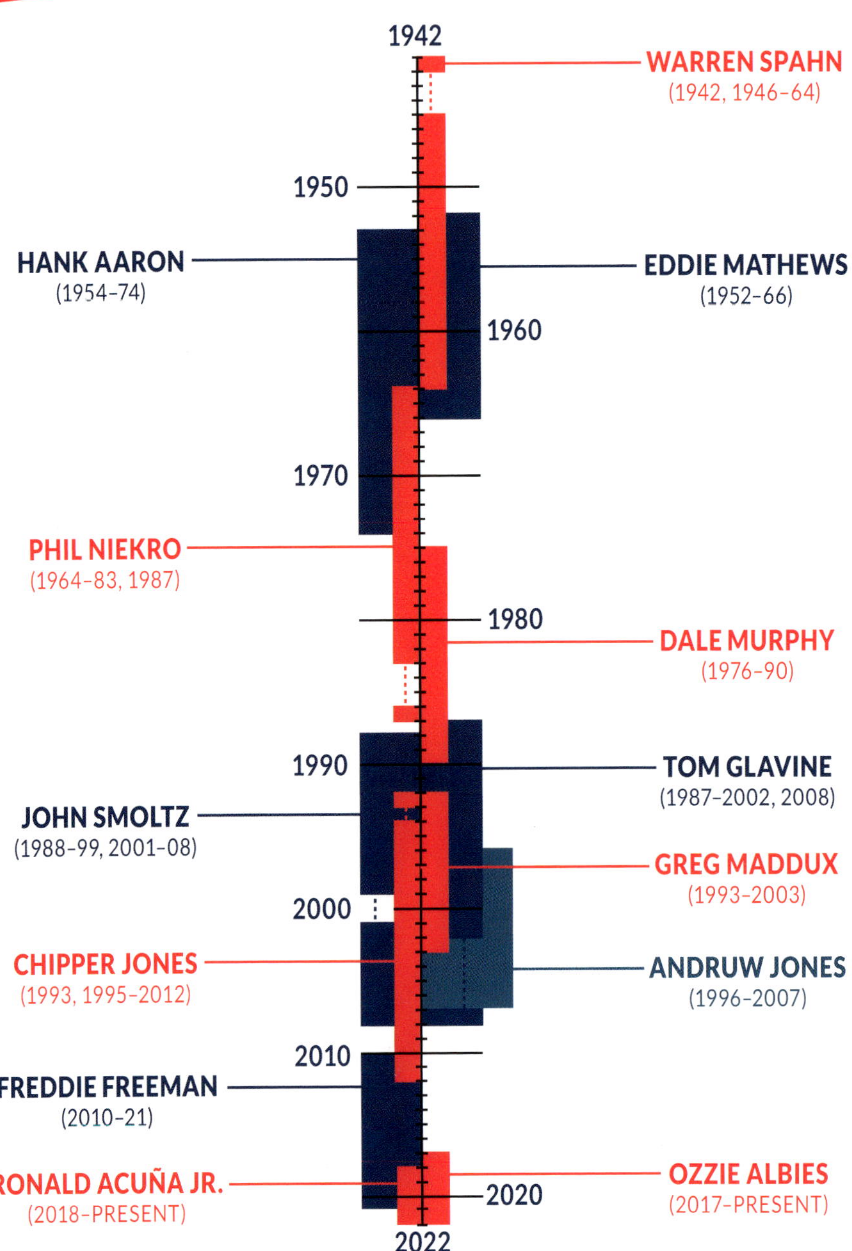

TEAM FACTS

ATLANTA BRAVES

Formerly: Boston (various nicknames, 1876–1952); Milwaukee Braves (1953–65)

World Series titles: 4 (1914, 1957, 1995, 2021)*

Key managers:

Bobby Cox (1978–81, 1990–2010)
2,149–1,709 (.557), 1 World Series title

Fred Haney (1956–59)
341–231 (.596), 1 World Series title

George Stallings (1913–20)
579–597 (.492), 1 World Series title

MORE INFORMATION

To learn more about the Atlanta Braves, go to **pressboxbooks.com/AllAccess**.

These links are routinely monitored and updated to provide the most current information available.

*1903 through 2022

GLOSSARY

baffled
Confused or puzzled.

consistent
Able to perform the same action over and over.

debut
First appearance.

dynamic
Energetic and exciting.

knuckleball
A pitch with little spin that moves unpredictably.

labor dispute
A disagreement between workers and their employers that can result in a work stoppage, such as a strike or lockout.

pennant
An American League or National League championship.

INDEX